# Magic Pony

## Annie Saves the Day

"We're looking for two other boys. One of them is wearing a green-and-black bike helmet. Seen them?"

"No," said Annie. "And if I had, I wouldn't tell you!"

Smudger's eyes narrowed dangerously.

"You'll tell me because I ask," he said, dropping his bike on the ground and advancing. He stretched his hand out to grab the reins but, before he could reach them, Ned lifted his head and flared his nostrils. He snorted a warning and stamped a front foot so hard the ground trembled.

**Join Annie on all her adventures
with Ned, the Magic Pony!**

# Magic Pony
## Annie Saves the Day

**Elizabeth Lindsay**

**Illustrated by John Eastwood**

A
**LITTLE APPLE**
PAPERBACK

SCHOLASTIC INC.
New York  Toronto  London  Auckland  Sydney
Mexico City  New Delhi  Hong Kong  Buenos Aires

*For Bridget*

ISBN 0-439-44651-1
Text copyright © 1998 Elizabeth Lindsay.
Illustrations copyright © 1998 John Eastwood.

All rights reserved. Published by Scholastic Inc., 557 Broadway, New York, NY 10012, by arrangement with Scholastic Children's Books, Scholastic Ltd. SCHOLASTIC, Little Apple, and associated logos are trademarks and/or registered trademarks of Scholastic Inc.

12 11 10 9 8 7 6 5 4 3 2 1          3 4 5 6 7 8/0

Printed in the U.S.A.
First Scholastic printing, February 2003

## Chapter 1

# A Pony in the Bedroom

Annie smiled at Tabitha in an absentminded sort of way, holding a white hairbrush. The tabby cat lay on the grass in a pool of sunshine, front paws stretched forward. She loved being groomed. Annie squinted into the light and pulled the brush along the cat's silky fur. Tabitha rolled onto her back, purring loudly. Keeping up gentle strokes, Annie let her thoughts drift indoors to the chestnut pony in the poster on her bedroom wall. It was not an ordinary poster. Ned — the pony in the picture — came to life and was Annie's biggest secret.

Every morning when Annie woke up, she looked to see if Ned was still there. If the poster was empty, the magic was working and an adventure was about to start. But Ned had remained in the poster for nearly a week, and when Annie woke up this morning he was still just a shiny, paper picture. She wished the magic could work every day and sighed a long sigh, wondering how many more days she would have to wait.

Her thoughts were interrupted by her brother, Jamie, and his friend Ben, skidding around the side of the house on their mountain bikes before squealing to a stop on the grass. Tabitha leaped to her feet and streaked to the garden fence, clawing her way up to perch out of reach.

"Jamie, did you have to do that?" Annie protested.

"I didn't do anything!" Jamie unclipped

the chin strap of his new green-and-black bike helmet before pulling it off. Both boys looked extremely pleased with themselves.

"What have you been up to?" Annie asked.

"Nothing much. Beat Smudger Evans in a bike race, that's all. Bet my new helmet that I would win — so it's lucky I did."

"Too bad Smudger doesn't agree." Ben

grinned. "He says he was first — but you won by a wheel and a half, easy."

Jamie tossed the new bike helmet to his friend and shrugged. "Smudger always lies to get what he wants, and he wants my helmet."

Ben tried it on. "He's very mad at you for not handing it over."

"Be careful," said Annie, remembering how big Smudger was. "He might steal it."

"I'll keep out of his way until he cools off. Anyway, Annie, did you know that Penelope Potter is in the field, jumping Pebbles?"

Annie scrambled to her feet, surprised. Before coming out to brush Tabitha, she

had lined up her three china ponies —
Esmerelda, Prince, and Percy — on her
bedroom windowsill, to look out over
Pebbles's field. Then, the dapple gray
pony had been quietly grazing.

"But Penelope told me she wasn't
riding today. She was going shopping
with her mom."

"If you don't believe me, go and look."

Although suspicious that he might be
teasing, Annie didn't need to be told
twice. She loved anything to do with
ponies, as Jamie well knew. Not that
Penelope was particularly generous with
Pebbles. She would let Annie muck out
the stable and clean Pebbles's tack
whenever she liked, but it was only rarely
that she let Annie ride him.

Annie raced around the house, flung
herself out of the side gate and across the

road, to find Penelope riding around the field at a steady canter. Pebbles did look handsome, his gray mane flying and his tail streaming silver in the breeze. Annie clambered up the bottom bar of the gate and leaned over to watch.

Penelope had set out a proper show-jumping course. There was a staircase, a crosspole double, a parallel, and, between each of these, a row of blue barrels, making six jumps in all.

*What kind of shopping with your mom*

*is that?* thought Annie, wrinkling her nose.

Pebbles flew over the staircase and cantered to a row of barrels. Annie knew he would clear everything by miles. He loved to jump, and Penelope was a very good rider. Pebbles pricked his ears at the crosspole double and cleared it and the next row of barrels easily. In no time at all, he was flying over the parallel, having

jumped the whole course. Penelope turned in a circle and stopped for a breather.

"Oh, hello," she said, noticing Annie on the gate.

"You didn't go shopping after all," said Annie.

"It's been changed to tomorrow," replied Penelope. "So I'm jumping instead."

"Can I have a turn?" The words were

out before Annie could stop them. There was a pause while Penelope looked down her nose and made a decision.

"Yes, all right," she said, swinging herself out of the saddle and offering the reins. "Take him around the show jumps." It was a dare.

"OK." And Annie took the reins.

It was obvious from Penelope's self-satisfied smirk that she expected Annie to fall flat on her face. But Annie's life had changed in a way Penelope knew nothing about. Since the day Annie bought the pony poster from Cosby's Magic Emporium, whenever Ned came to life — whether he was a pony the same size as Pebbles or as tiny as Percy, the smallest of her three china ponies — he had been teaching Annie to ride.

"I guess you should have my hat," said

Penelope, pulling it off and handing it over.

"Thanks."

Annie put on the riding hat and did up the chin strap, ignoring the warning voice in her head that said *don't jump*. Instead, aching to ride again, she swung herself into the saddle. So Penelope expected her to fall off, did she? Well, she'd show her!

Annie took a deep breath and squeezed Pebbles with her legs. Being a willing pony, it was all he needed, and they were soon trotting across the grass. Annie decided to take the same jumping route as Penelope. At least Pebbles would know what he was doing, even if she didn't. She sat up, gave him another squeeze, and they were all too quickly cantering for the first row of barrels.

They were in the air when Annie caught sight of Penelope's astonished face and realized she had made a terrible mistake. Yes, her riding had improved, but Penelope would want to know why and how. It was too late to stop and they cantered on toward the staircase. As they passed the gate, Annie glimpsed a movement in her bedroom window and turned for a better look. Behind the windowpane, a full-sized chestnut pony shook his head.

With Annie's attention suddenly elsewhere, a moment of terrible confusion followed. Annie expected Pebbles to jump, but the pony stopped dead to find out what she was looking at. Annie sailed over the staircase by herself, somersaulting spectacularly, to land on

the other side with a jarring bump. For a moment she lay on the ground winded, then rolled over to find Penelope looking up at her bedroom window, too. Fortunately, the full-sized chestnut pony had gone, and instead of three china ponies on the windowsill, she counted four. That was lucky.

"Well, you cleared it," Penelope said, unsympathetically, hauling Annie up. "You really should look where you're going. What were you looking at, anyway?"

"Nothing," said Annie. "You might ask if I'm all right."

"Well, are you?"

"I suppose so."

"In that case, give me my hat back." Penelope held out her hand. "I thought you'd fall off at the first jump. Have you been taking lessons?"

"Beginner's luck," said Annie hastily. "I learned from watching you."

"Very lucky. I'm surprised you managed to stay on for so long. You haven't been riding Pebbles when I'm not here, have you?"

"Of course not!"

"I can't think of how else you could have improved." Penelope did up her chin strap and got the dappled pony, who was quietly nibbling grass. "I'm going out for a ride. Open the gate, will you?"

Annie was overcome with regret at having given some of her secret away and quickly pulled back the bolt. Penelope rode into the road, leaving Annie to close the gate behind her.

"You could come with me, if you like," Penelope said. "Borrow Jamie's bike to keep up. I'd lend you mine, only I don't want it to get dirty."

"No — no — I can't," stuttered Annie. "There's something I've got to do."

"Suit yourself," said Penelope. Then as an afterthought she added, "You've got a grass stain on your jeans." She set off at a trot along the road to Winchway Wood without so much as a backward look.

"I'll never be so careless again," Annie promised herself, darting through the side gate. "Penelope must never find out about Ned."

And she raced around the side of the house, determined to get to her bedroom as fast as possible.

## Chapter 2

# Green Bottom

Annie saw Jamie's bike at the last minute. It lay on the grass in front of her, and she made a flying leap to clear it. On landing, her sneakers slipped out from under her, and for the second time that day she landed on her bottom — *ouch!* — and slid across the grass.

Jamie hurried out the back door, his friend Ben following.

"Watch my bike!" he said.

"What do you mean, watch your bike! You left it in the middle of the lawn for people to trip over." Annie got up, stretching her leg. "That hurt."

Ben creeped up behind her. "You've got a green bottom." He grinned.

"What do you expect!" Annie noticed Ben's bike propped against the shed. She turned on her brother. "If you did what Ben did and put your bike out of the way, accidents wouldn't happen. I could have broken my leg."

"Make her invisible, Jamie," said Ben.

"Good idea."

Jamie pulled on his green-and-black helmet, then zapped well-practiced magician's magic hands under Annie's nose and waggled them around her head. "Split splat vanish," he commanded.

"Stop that!" Annie ran for the back door.

"See? Works every time!" Jamie said, and Ben laughed.

"You think you're a magician, Jamie? You don't know the first thing about magic, so there!" Annie yelled from the safety of the kitchen.

"Green bottom, green bottom, green bottom," chanted the boys, making faces.

"What's going on?" asked Mom, coming in from the living room. "Oh, Annie! Look at the state of your jeans. They were clean this morning."

"I just tripped over Jamie's bike," complained Annie. "It wasn't my fault. He left it in the middle of the lawn."

Nevertheless, she could see that falling over the bike had been a piece of luck. Now she could explain her green bottom without having to say she fell off Pebbles — something she would rather keep to herself.

"That's enough, boys," said Mom. Still laughing, Jamie and Ben swung themselves onto their bikes and pedaled off around the side of the house.

"So what are you going to do now, Annie?" Mom asked. "You could help me bake a cake."

"No, no, I've got something important

to do in my bedroom." Mom gave her a curious look. Annie usually jumped at the opportunity to help with the baking. "I do. Honest!"

"Well — if you're sure."

Annie scooted to the hall. Everything was becoming more complicated by the minute.

By the time she arrived in her bedroom, even seeing the tiny Ned canter along the windowsill didn't alter the fact that, so far, the day was going badly. She'd given away part of her biggest secret to Penelope, she had nearly had a fight with Jamie, and Mom was wondering what could possibly be more important than making a cake.

"Hello, Ned," she said. "Everything's going horribly wrong." And, as if to prove it, she tripped over a book lying on the carpet and fell across the bedspread with a grunt. "See what I mean?"

In almost as much time as it takes to blink, Ned jumped from the windowsill and changed size. Annie found herself pulled upright in a gentle but firm manner by Ned's strong teeth holding her sweatshirt.

"So," said the pony, blowing on her cheek. "What's up?" He wobbled his lips

against her hand. "There's no need to look so miserable."

"I should never have ridden Pebbles," cried Annie. "I did it to show off and . . ." She didn't finish.

"And what?" asked Ned.

"Because I missed you. When you're in the poster and I can't talk to you and we don't go riding, I get lonely. I know I've got

Mom and Dad and Jamie and Tabitha, but it's not the same as a magic pony."

"Mmm," said Ned, giving it some thought. "You don't want to arouse people's suspicions by riding too well, that's true. But by falling off in the end, you did what Penelope expected. Don't worry, she'll quickly forget. She's that sort of person. As for me, I come when I come and I go when I go. We both have to make the best of that. Magic is strange stuff."

"Then I fell over Jamie's bike and he and his friend Ben laughed at me. And Mom wanted me to help make a cake and now she's wondering why I didn't."

"What you need is a nice long ride in the woods. That will make things better," said Ned.

"Yes," cried Annie, flinging her arms around his neck and burying her face in

his chestnut mane. "I'd love that more than anything."

"Then please make some tiny steps up to the windowsill. Can you do that?"

"Oh, yes," said Annie. She was sure she could.

"Then you'll need to open the window, get on my back, and I will make us both tiny. Then we'll climb the steps and jump down to the garden by way of the fig tree."

"How exciting," cried Annie, and squeezed behind Ned's hindquarters to rummage under the bed. She pulled out a tattered cardboard box.

"I can make steps with these," she said. "They're building blocks, from when I was little." And she tipped out a pile of red, yellow, green, and blue plastic bricks and began sticking them together. Ned looked on with interest until they heard the sound of footsteps coming up the stairs. In a moment, the big Ned was gone and the tiny Ned cantered under the bed. By the time Mom opened the door, he had disappeared.

"Goodness," she said. "I thought you'd given up playing with those long ago."

"I have really, only I'm making steps for Esmerelda, Prince, and Percy in case they want to come off the windowsill," said Annie, saying the first thing that came into her head.

"I see," said Mom, looking at the line of china ponies. "Well, I've come to tell you I've decided to make the cake later. Instead, I'm going into the garden, in case you wonder where I am. There's some digging to do in the vegetable patch. So we can still make the cake together, if you like."

"I do like," said Annie. "Later."

Mom laughed. "Good luck with the steps. I hope Esmerelda, Prince, and Percy are truly grateful." And the door closed behind her.

Annie's nimble fingers worked quickly. She was already planning how she would tape the top of the Lego stairs to her windowsill and wedge them in place with books at the sides. By the time Ned cantered out from under the bed, the steps were almost completed.

"How are you doing?" he asked in his tinkly bell tiny voice.

"Nearly done."

Once she'd heaved the books from her shelf, Annie's construction didn't take too long to finish. The miniature staircase was the perfect size for a tiny pony. She was putting the last piece of tape in place when the big Ned leaned his muzzle on her shoulder.

"Open the window and get on," he said, standing tacked up and ready.

Laughing with excitement, Annie flung the window wide open before squeezing between Ned and the wall.

"It's hard to get on in such a small bedroom."

Somehow, she managed to put a foot in the stirrup and slide up the wall before swinging her leg over. The moment she touched the saddle, there was a rush of wind and the space around them was suddenly huge. Annie's jeans and sweatshirt were gone and in their place were her magic riding clothes — black velvet hard hat, jacket, jodhpurs and jodhpur boots, shirt, and tie — which turned her into a person nobody recognized. Ned trotted across the carpet toward the staircase. It stretched high above them.

"Now," said Ned. "Keep hold of the reins and get off. You're going to lead me up."

"But it's so high," gasped Annie. "There are sixty-eight steps. I counted."

"Then the sooner we start, the sooner we'll reach the top! But remember, don't let go of the reins, otherwise you'll grow big and demolish everything."

"Don't worry, I won't."

Annie slid to the ground and lifted the reins over Ned's head.

"Off you go," he said. "I'll follow right behind."

Keeping a tight hold, Annie started to climb. The stairs seemed to go up and up forever, and she didn't dare look down in case she felt dizzy and fell off. Sixty-eight steps later, she arrived at the windowsill so winded that she didn't look where she was going and bumped right into Percy.

"Sorry." She apologized automatically, but, of course, Percy, being china, just stood there. She stepped around him and led the way to the window, peeping outside. When she was a big person, it was a long way down. Now that she was tiny, the ground was miles away.

"Are we really going to jump down there?"

"We certainly are," said Ned. "Get on."

Annie did as she was told, lifting the reins back over Ned's head, although her knees were wobbling so much she could hardly put her foot in the stirrup.

"Don't worry about a thing," said Ned, giving her a helping shove with his nose. But Annie was scared. She couldn't help it.

Ned stepped through the open window and, the closer they came to the drop, the more frightened she became.

## Chapter 3

# Ride Like the Wind

Both Annie's hands grabbed handfuls of mane and she hung on.

"No, no, that won't do," said Ned. "Take hold of the reins and relax. You'll soon learn to balance."

With reluctance, Annie let go and took the reins as she was told. The moment she did so, Ned jumped. Annie

gasped at the daring of it.
When they landed on
a fig leaf, instead of the
great bump she expected,
the sturdy green platform
dipped and rose, flexing gently. What a
relief! Ned balanced himself as if on a
springboard, and all the while Annie
found herself nodding up and down like
some kind of a jack-in-a-box. It was such
a funny feeling, it made her giggle.

Then they were in the air again and
landing on the leaf below. Each leaf
became a swaying step and Ned dropped
from one to another all the way down the
tree. When they landed on the grass, it
was with an unexpected thud that shot
Annie halfway up Ned's neck. She
pushed herself back in the saddle.

"Scary, but fun?" asked Ned.

"Scary, but fun," agreed Annie.

Thanks to Dad having just cut it, the grass was short and springy. Ned stepped from one lush blade to the next with an easy stride.

"Are we going to stay small all the way during our ride?" Annie asked.

"Certainly not," said Ned. "Once we get to the road, it'll be safe to grow big. Then we can really get going." He stepped onto the front path.

"But if we stay small, how are we going to open the gate?" Annie asked, looking up to the latch, which seemed as high as the sky.

"There's a way through at the bottom. Part of that plank's rotted. The gap's just big enough for us to squeeze through."

"Oh, yes!"

"Don't forget to duck."

Ned trotted briskly forward. Annie was glad for the warning, for the gap was low and narrow. She pulled in her arms and crouched. Ned was about to go

through when a squeal of bike brakes in the road stopped him.

"Knock on the front door, Henry. See if they're inside."

"Hold tight," said Ned, and charged for the flower bed. He was just in time.

The gate swung open and a pair of feet clomped up the path. They heard a rat-a-tat-tat on the front door.

"It's Smudger Evans!" whispered Annie, peering out from underneath a marigold. "That other boy's Henry, one of his gang. Smudger's after Jamie's new bike helmet."

"Is he?" said Ned.

"Smudger says Jamie owes it to him after losing a bike race. Only Jamie says he didn't lose, he won. But Smudger's like that. He tells lies. And now he's got his friends together."

There was no answer at the front door and Henry clomped back down the path.

Obviously Mom was digging in the vegetable garden and didn't hear.

"No one's in, Smudger," Henry said, not bothering to shut the gate.

Annie could see Smudger's mean face and, behind Smudger, leaning on their handlebars, the skinny twins, Nick and Stew.

"Probably in the woods. A good place to catch up with them. I want that helmet. Jamie Deakin owes it to me."

"That's right, Smudger," said Henry. "You tell him."

"I'm not telling him, Henry," sneered Smudger. "I'm taking it." Smudger stood on his pedals and set off down the lane. The skinny twins said nothing, just nodded knowingly and tagged after their leader.

"Yeah, that's right," said Henry, leaping onto his bike and hurrying to catch up.

"It's not fair!" said Annie. "That's four against two. Jamie and Ben don't stand a chance. We've got to warn them."

"We will," said Ned, trotting back to the road and straight into a wild wind. It spun them big in a moment. Now Annie was sitting higher than the gate and, as Ned walked forward to the road, she was able to lean over and pull it shut behind them.

Hot on the trail of Smudger and the gang, Ned set off at a brisk trot toward Winchway Wood. Annie kept time with her best up-down, up-down rising trot, and wondered where they should look first for her brother and his friend.

Where the road ended, Ned turned into the woods and, the moment his feet touched earth, he broke into a rhythmic canter. Across the path lay the log they had jumped once before. Now it held no terrors for Annie and, after Ned had cleared it, she urged him forward until they were galloping so fast that the wind whistled. They quickly reached the top of the slope where the path curled out of sight between the trees.

Here Ned slowed down, and they found themselves trotting into an overhung gully edged with gnarled and twisted roots. Tire marks snaked high up the bank's sandy soil.

"Jamie and Ben?" wondered Annie. "Or Smudger and his gang?"

"We'll go on," said Ned. From nowhere, two bikes swerved across the path ahead.

Ned half reared and Annie gasped. It was Smudger and Henry, and behind them, skidding to cut off their retreat, came the skinny twins, Nick and Stew. Annie swallowed nervously.

"It's just a girl on a pony," said Henry.

"But there were two voices," said Smudger suspiciously.

"Clear the path, please," said Annie. "I need to get by."

"You seen anyone else around here?" Henry asked.

"No," said Annie. "Only those two." And she pointed at Nick and Stew.

"Not them," said Smudger. "We know them. We're looking for two other boys. One of them is wearing a green-and-black bike helmet. Seen them?"

"No," said Annie. "And if I had, I wouldn't tell you!"

Smudger's eyes narrowed dangerously.

"You'll tell me because I ask," he said, dropping his bike on the ground and advancing. He stretched his hand out to grab the reins but, before he could reach them, Ned lifted his head and flared his nostrils. He snorted a warning and stamped a front foot so hard the ground trembled. Smudger backed off.

"You keep that nag under control," he said.

Ned didn't like being called a nag or the tone of Smudger's voice, and he let out an angry whinny, rearing up to slice the air with his front legs. Smudger dived for safety and Ned leaped toward Smudger's bike. Annie clung on, and Henry, fearing the worst, quickly pulled his bike to one side, then scrambled up the bank. But Ned didn't trample

Smudger's bike, he jumped it and galloped out of the gully, raising a dust cloud behind them.

"That should give them something to think about," he said when they were out of hearing.

"It did," said Annie, aware of the four startled faces left behind and relieved she hadn't fallen off.

It wasn't until they were calmly cantering between the trees that she realized not one of the boys had recognized her — thanks to the wonderful riding clothes disguise.

## Chapter 4

# Ambush

Annie and Ned reached the highest point in the woods and took the opportunity to look around. In one direction, the trees sloped all the way down to the river. They glimpsed the path that wove along the riverbank, the water glinting in the sunlight, the far bank edged with trees and the grassy field beyond.

But there was no sign of Jamie or Ben. The only sound was a trilling blackbird. Even Smudger and his gang seemed to have been swallowed up by the trees. But they were there, lurking. Annie was sure they were doing exactly what she and Ned were doing — searching for Jamie.

"Annie, think," said Ned. "Where do Jamie and Ben really like to go when they bike in the woods?"

"They ride the Ups and Downs, which is a track that goes around in a twisty loop and up and down a lot."

"I guessed it might," said Ned.

"Or they could have gone to the rope swing down by the river. But the Ups and Downs are nearest."

"We'll try there first, then," said Ned. "Which way?"

"Along the ridge and then drop down.

The Ups and Downs are in a sort of valley."

Ned cantered along the ridge and Annie kept a cautious lookout. They met the path that sloped toward the Ups and Downs, and Ned slowed to a walk. They listened for telltale voices but heard nothing until grunts of effort, the whir of

bicycle chains, and the click of gears gave away the fact that someone was biking down below.

Annie guided Ned between the trees to the top of a steep slope, where they took cover in the undergrowth.

"See, down there. There's the bendy path where the bikes go around."

Taking care not to be seen, they peeped into the valley. Smudger was the first biker they saw, pedaling slowly up a hill and down again. The skinny twins followed, and an unsteady Henry brought up the rear.

"They're still looking," said Ned. "They're not giving up, are they?"

"Doesn't look like it," replied Annie. "Do you think we should go down and look, too?"

"Just to make sure," said Ned.

Turning away from the steep slope ahead, they made their way into the valley by the path. Annie didn't feel as frightened about meeting Smudger now, but, given a choice, she would rather not.

It was obvious when they reached the Ups and Downs. Tires had worn the path wide and smooth, fraying any protruding tree roots. Keeping a sharp lookout, they climbed and twisted and turned around the looping track. But by the time they arrived back where they started from, they had seen no one.

"Vanished," said Annie. "Not even a glimpse of Smudger and the gang."

"We've missed them all somehow," said Ned. "Better check the rope swing."

"Yes," said Annie, really anxious now. "We've wasted too much time looking after they've already gone. Smudger's got a head start on us now."

Ned swung around and set off, back up the valley slope to the higher part of the wood. Cantering along the ridge, Annie turned him, searching the path that led down to the river. But, even though she looked for it, she couldn't find it.

"I'm lost," she admitted at last. Ned skidded to a stop. Unconcerned voices drifted up between the trees. Shouts and laughter and friendly banter. "It's Jamie and Ben."

"Yes," said Ned. "And making enough noise to guide Smudger right to them."

"Quick," said Annie. "We've got to get there first."

"The voices are straight ahead," said Ned. "The river must be down this way."

"I'm not sure," said Annie. "I think we

need to double back a little way to find the path."

"We don't have time to double back. Smudger and the others could be there by now."

Ned cantered straight toward the voices, although they couldn't see the river or the great oak tree with its swinging rope. He was forced to slow down when they found themselves funneled into a path between sharp brambles that twisted and turned and took them up, not down.

"This is no good," said Ned, unable to turn back because the path was so narrow. Then, unexpectedly, they emerged onto a rocky plateau. "Where are we now?"

"This is where Mom and Dad come blackberry picking," said Annie, realizing the horrible truth of it. "We're on the cliff. We can't get down to the river from here. It's a precipice. We've got to go back."

Looking below, her eye caught something swinging between the trees. Ned stepped a little closer to the edge and they looked down over the brambles. They could see the river and Jamie, swinging out across the water on a rope.

"Now what do we do?" asked Annie. Ben sat on a tree root, his feet idly dangling in the flow. "This is hopeless." The boys' bikes leaned against the far side of the broad oak, and hanging from one of the saddles, was Jamie's new green-and-black bike helmet. "The helmet! Why isn't he wearing it?" Annie groaned. "Why's he swinging when he should be keeping a lookout?"

"Because he doesn't know that Smudger and his friends are after him," said Ned grimly.

The words were no sooner said than
Smudger and the gang arrived — not on
their bikes, but creeping close to the
ground, out of sight. It was Henry who
spotted the helmet. He gave a wave and
pointed. Smudger signaled to the others
to retreat and stood up.

Annie couldn't control herself any longer and, rising in the stirrups, took a deep breath.

"Jamie!" she yelled. "Watch out!"

Startled pigeons burst between the branches and a jay shrieked a warning. Swinging out across the water, Jamie turned in time to see Smudger snatch the green-and-black helmet and run.

"Quick, Ben, grab him!"

But Ben scrambled up the bank too

late. By the time he reached the bikes, Smudger had the helmet on his head and was leaping onto his own bike, which Stew held ready for him. With victorious whoops, the four boys pedaled off, leaving Jamie to jump to the bank and angrily kick a tree root. Annie slumped back into the saddle in despair.

"Now what do we do?" she asked.

## Chapter 5

# Splash! Splash!

Ned reared up and spun around, almost landing Annie in a bramble bush. Somehow she stayed on.

"We cut them off," he said. "That's what we do. Hold tight."

Annie grabbed a handful of mane as Ned twisted and turned along the narrow bramble path and galloped back between the trees, slithering down toward the river path to cut off the gang's escape. Annie saw the boys glide between the trees, laughing, shouting, victorious, with the green-and-black bike helmet fastened on Smudger's head.

Ned cantered onto the path, ears flat back, and galloped straight toward them.

Smudger was the first to see him and spun to a startled halt. The twins stopped behind him, but Henry had to swerve and ended up in a heap.

"Back!" shouted Smudger. "Back the other way. It's that girl and her maniac pony."

The boys turned and quickly retreated the way they had come. Henry struggled to his feet and, with an alarmed look over his shoulder, raced to get away.

"We've got to stop them. They could escape across the bridge," said Annie. "It takes you over the river to the field."

"Where is the bridge?" Ned asked.

"It's where the path bends. A wooden platform sort of bridge. Right there!"

No sooner had Annie explained than the bridge came into view, and cantering toward it across the field was Penelope Potter on Pebbles. Jamie and Ben, pedaling furiously, had almost reached it, too, and shouted gleefully when they saw Smudger had changed direction and was heading back toward them. Even though Smudger was going his fastest to get there first, it seemed to Annie that everyone was going to arrive at the bridge at the same time.

Penelope and Pebbles had just started across when Smudger turned his bike onto the planks. Jamie and Ben were almost upon him, and Smudger was desperate to lead his gang to safety. But the bridge was too narrow for a bike and pony to pass one another.

"Get out of the way," yelled Smudger. "I've got to get over!"

"Don't be silly," shouted Penelope. "Horses have the right-of-way." And, as Smudger tried to push past, she took her foot from the stirrup and gave him a shove.

Smudger completely lost his balance, and bike and boy toppled into the water with a mighty splash. Unfortunately for Penelope, the splash startled Pebbles so much that he half reared and jumped for the bank between the remaining gang members. Penelope also lost her balance and, with a cry of dismay, toppled over the other side of the bridge.

Another splash was too much for Pebbles. Seeing the path for home, he bolted down it and came galloping toward Annie and Ned, reins and stirrups flying. Annie just had time to see Jamie jump in to help Penelope before Ned whinnied and turned to keep pace with the frightened Pebbles.

"Take hold of his reins, Annie," Ned said. Annie stretched out to grab them — not so easy when going full speed and trying to keep her balance. It seemed like forever before she managed to close her hand around them.

"Whoa, Pebbles," she said. "Steady, boy."

At last Pebbles slowed.

"Good pony, good boy," said Annie in her most soothing tone. "Good fella."

By the time they came to a stop, Pebbles was no longer showing the whites of his eyes and, although snorting heavily, seemed calmer.

"I don't blame you for being frightened by the splashes," soothed Annie, stroking his neck.

Ned turned and the ponies trotted back side by side along the path.

"No one's going to recognize me, are they?" she asked.

"They certainly are not," said Ned. "Trust your disguise, Annie. You'll be a stranger to them all."

She hoped Ned was right.

Nearing the bridge, they were treated to quite a sight. The water flowed at shoulder height, and everyone in it was thoroughly soaked. Penelope was being pushed onto the bridge by Jamie and was shouting furious insults at Smudger. On the other side, the skinny twins were trying unsuccessfully to help Smudger lift his bike from the water.

"I still don't see how we're going to get Jamie's helmet back," said Annie.

"You offer to pull out Smudger's bike in return for it," said Ned, keeping his voice low so as not to be heard by the others.

Once Penelope was out of the water, the skinny twins jumped away to keep out of reach of her flailing riding crop. On the bank, Henry was hopping from one foot to the other, uncertain of what to do, and Ben was holding his and Jamie's bikes, ready to defend them against any

threat. To attract Penelope's attention, Ned whinnied loudly.

"My pony," she cried when she saw them. "Pebbles!" She gave one last swipe and squelched across the bridge. When she reached Annie, she took the offered reins. "He bolted," she said, as if Annie didn't know. "Lucky you were passing. That idiotic boy in the water frightened him. I'm soaked." She turned to Jamie, who stood dripping behind her. "Thank you, Jamie, you're a hero," she said and swung herself into the saddle. "I'm going home before I catch pneumonia."

And Penelope scowled one last time at Smudger before turning Pebbles and setting off for home in a very bad mood.

"Everyone all right?" Annie asked brightly when Penelope was gone.

"Just a little wet," said Jamie, with a

shy smile. "OK, Smudger, give me back my bike helmet."

"Yes, give him back his bike helmet," said Annie. Everyone turned to look at her. Smudger's bike slipped back into the water for the umpteenth time, and his teeth started to chatter. "And I'll get my pony to pull your bike out of the river."

"It's a deal," said the miserable Smudger.

"Helmet first," said Jamie, shooting a grateful look in Annie's direction. Smudger undid the chin strap and tossed the helmet to Jamie. Jamie pulled it on and fastened it.

"Excuse me, but how did you know he'd stolen my helmet?" he asked.

"Oh, when our paths crossed earlier, he wasn't wearing one," Annie said simply.

"Pass the rope, then," said Jamie.

*Rope!* thought Annie and realized that until this moment she hadn't given a thought to how she was going to do the pulling. She looked behind her to where a coil was fastened to the saddle. It hadn't been there earlier, but she knew better than to question Ned's magic. He pawed the ground impatiently until she untied it and tossed one end to Jamie. She tied her end around Ned's neck. Jamie threw

the rope to Smudger, and, when it was fastened around the handlebars, Ned turned and pulled. The bike glided through the water to the bank. Henry and the skinny twins lifted it clear of a tree root, and it was back on dry land. Jamie undid the knot while the twins took a hand each and hauled Smudger up the bank. He nodded in Annie's direction.

"Thanks."

"Not at all," said Annie, coiling the rope and tying it back to the saddle. Jamie took his bike from Ben.

"Yes, thanks very much," he said. Annie couldn't help a grin, thrilled that even her own brother hadn't recognized her in her magic riding clothes.

"Glad to have helped," she said, wondering how Jamie was going to explain his soaking clothes to Mom. "Good-bye."

Ned set off at a steady trot toward home and Jamie and Ben pedaled after them, leaving the gang to see if their leader's bike was damaged.

"Hold tight," said Ned. "We'd better get a move on. We've got to get back before Jamie and Ben." He broke into an exhilarating gallop that ate up the ground, and he didn't slow down until they came out of the wood onto the road. When they reached Annie's front gate, the rushing wind spun them tiny again. They squeezed through the gap at the bottom of the gate and were across the grass in no time. Jumping up the fig-tree leaves was much less frightening than jumping down. Besides, Annie was feeling more confident after her ride.

They reached the windowsill just as Jamie and Ben coasted up to the side gate, where they said a happy good-bye to each other. Ned quickly stepped over the sill to the safety of Annie's bedroom.

"What an adventure," she said, dismounting and giving Ned a big hug. "Thank you for saving the day."

"We did it together." Ned tossed his head. "No need to go down the steps. Just let go of the reins and jump." Annie did so without thinking and leaped into a whirling wind. In a flash, she was standing next to the Lego steps, her full size again, once more wearing her sweatshirt, jeans, and sneakers. As for Ned, he was back in his picture.

Outside, she heard the whir of bicycle tires on the lane. A dripping Smudger Evans, trailed by his forlorn gang, was pedaling for home.

"It really was a wonderful adventure, Ned," she said, wistfully running her finger across the glossy pony poster. "Jamie got his bike helmet back, and not one of them guessed it was me."

Then she opened the door and hurried downstairs. From the living room, she could see Mom and Jamie on the grass. She darted into the kitchen and put her head around the back door.

"Can we make the cake now?" she asked and then, with an impish grin, said, "Oh, Jamie. You're all wet."

"Don't you start," Jamie said. "I fell in the river. OK? But it was worth it."

"Some argument about his bike helmet," said Mom, shaking her head. "Now go on upstairs and get in the bath."

"Mom, don't make a fuss."

"I'm not. I don't want you getting a cold, that's all."

"Can I get the cake things out?" Annie asked. "And can it be a chocolate one?"

"If you want," said Mom. "I'll lock up the shed and we can start." Jamie sat on the step and pulled off his waterlogged sneakers.

"Can it have chocolate icing?" he said.

"I'll ask Mom. I know there's a package of chocolate chips in the cupboard."

"Yum," said Jamie. "I'll help decorate it when I've taken my bath. Oh, and I'll tell you how I beat Smudger Evans and his gang. Me, Ben, Penelope Potter, and this mystery girl on a chestnut pony."

"Oh?"

"Yes, you'll never believe what happened. It was amazing."

And he padded into the living room, leaving Annie to open a bag of flour and smile a secret smile.